Phoebe Gilman

Little Blue Ben

Author: Gilman, Phoebe.
Reading Level: 2.0 LG
Point Value: 0.5
ACCELERATED READER QUIZ 45272

 # Little Blue Ben

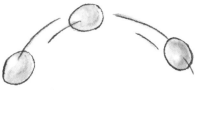

Scholastic Canada Ltd.

Toronto New York London Auckland Sydney
Mexico City New Delhi Hong Kong Buenos Aires

Scholastic Canada Ltd.
175 Hillmount Road, Markham, Ontario L6C 1Z7, Canada

Scholastic Inc.
555 Broadway, New York, NY 10012, USA

Scholastic Australia Pty Limited
PO Box 579, Gosford, NSW 2250, Australia

Scholastic New Zealand Limited
Private Bag 94407, Greenmount, Auckland, New Zealand

Scholastic Ltd.
Villiers House, Clarendon Avenue, Leamington Spa,
Warwickshire CV32 5PR, UK

Library and Archives Canada Cataloguing in Publication

Gilman, Phoebe, 1940-2002
Little Blue Ben / Phoebe Gilman.

First published in 1986.
ISBN 0-439-96163-7

1. Children's poetry, Canadian (English) I. Title.

PS8563.I54L58 2005   jC811'.54   C2004-904930-5

6 5 4 3 2 1   Printed in Singapore   05 06 07 08

Little Blue Ben
lives in the glen

with his brother, Blue Cat,
and their mother, Blue Hen.

Their little blue house
is filled to the door
with eggs the hen lays
by the dozens and more.

She boils eggs for breakfast,
she fries eggs for lunch.
For supper she toasts them
to give them a crunch.

"Just wait till you taste
this new treat for the tummy.
These shish kebabed eggs
are deliciously yummy."

"Oh, yuck!" says Blue Ben.
"These eggs are *not* yummy!
They're sticky and icky.
They're bluey. They're crummy!"

"Let's play hide and seek,
and when I am the winner,
then *you'll* have to eat
my blue eggs for your dinner."
As little Blue Ben
disappears in the book,
search high and low
to help the cat look.

"Little Blue Ben,
I know you're not far.

Come out, come out,
wherever you are!"

"He must have gone this way.
He's sure to be near.

I'll never give up,
if it takes me all year."

"Where, oh where
can he possibly be?

Is he under that mushroom
or inside this tree?"

"Would he hide in the water?
How dumb can he get?

He can't be in there.
It's too cold. It's too wet."

"He's here in the grass . . .
No, he's under that stone.

I missed him again,"
says the cat with a moan.

"He won't ever find me," says Ben, full of glee.

"Who's tinier? Who's tougher? Who's trickier than me?"

"Ho, ho! I'm the greatest!
I knew I'd be winner!

Guess who'll be eating
blue eggs for his dinner?"

"Not I!" says the cat.
"All my troubles are past.
Little Blue Ben,
I've found you at last."

But they make such a noise
with their quarrelling then,
that it reaches the ears
of the wise old Blue Hen.

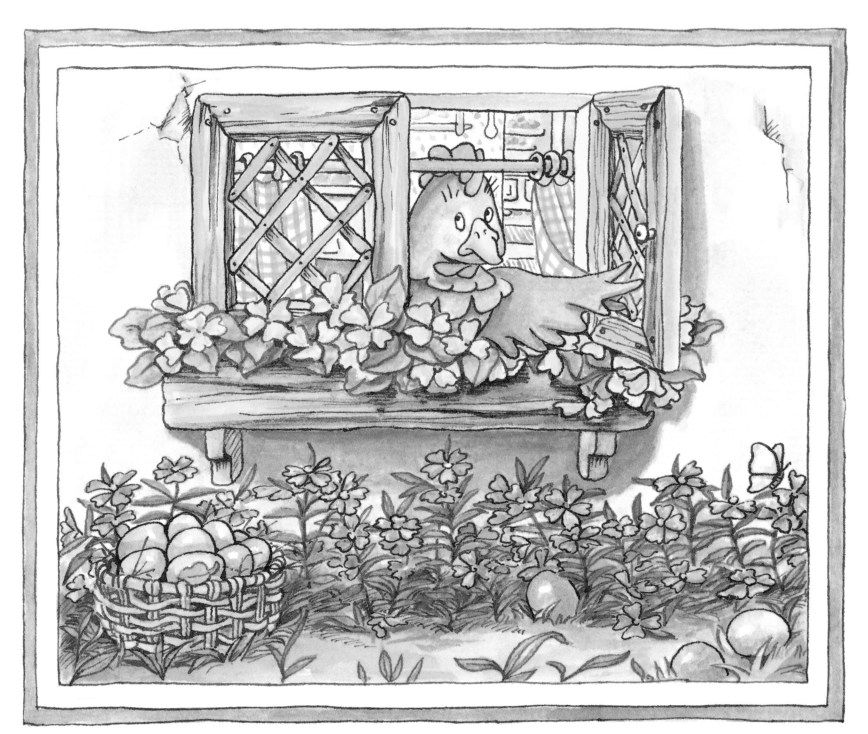

"I'm ashamed of you both
for making me scold.
Where have you been?
Your eggs are all cold."

"If you don't eat your eggs,
you won't grow up to be
as big and as strong
and as clever as me!"

Then Little Blue Ben,
and Blue Pussycat too,
are marched up to bed . . .

Goodbye. Toodle-oo!